D1302343

First published in this edition 1991

Published by Peter Haddock Ltd.
Bridlington, England.

Printed and bound in the United Kingdom

The Prickly Hedgehog

Snezana Pejacovic
Illustrated by Bojana Ban

“I am a prickly hedgehog! I have just woken from a long sleep, and I am sullen and angry, mean and moody.

Woe betide those who cross my path.”

"Leave us alone, you prickly hedgehog," cried the birds. "Don't you know that the swallows and storks are the heralds of spring? We don't like the sullen and the angry or the mean and the moody. We are in a hurry to tell the world that spring has arrived."

"I am a prickly hedgehog! I have just woken from a long sleep and I don't care about spring. I am sullen and angry, mean and moody.

Woe betide those who cross my path."

"Leave us alone, you prickly hedgehog," answered the fawn. "Spring is the time for the bear to pick berries, for the fawn to eat the new leaves and for the squirrels to climb amongst the green branches. Spring is not for the sullen and the angry, the mean and the moody."

“I am a prickly hedgehog! I have just woken from a long sleep and I do not care for spring, nor for berries, leaves and climbing. I am sullen and angry, mean and moody.

Woe betide those who cross my path.”

"Leave us alone, you prickly hedgehog," said the hares. "Spring is the time for us to dig our gardens and to weed and water them, not for looking at the sullen and the angry, the mean and the moody."

"I am a prickly hedgehog! I have just woken from a long sleep and I do not care for spring, berries, leaves and climbing, nor for digging gardens. I am sullen and angry, mean and moody.

Woe betide
those who
cross my path."

"Don't bother us, you prickly hedgehog," said the beaver. "Spring is the time for beavers, the famous builders, to build a new house. Our old one collapsed under the weight of the snow, and we have no time for the sullen and the angry, the mean and the moody."

"I am a prickly hedgehog! I have just woken from a long sleep and I do not care for spring, berries, leaves and climbing, digging gardens and building houses. I am sullen and angry, mean and moody.

Woe betide those who cross my path."

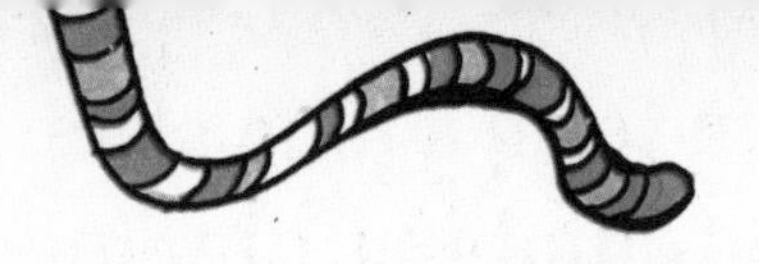

“Be off with you, you prickly hedgehog,” cried the mice. “Spring is for celebrating the return of the warm sun with the song of the birds, the music and dancing of mice and the sunbathing of lizards, and not for listening to the sullen and the angry, the mean and the moody.”

"I am a prickly hedgehog! I have just woken from a long sleep and I do not care for spring, berries, leaves and climbing, digging gardens and building houses, nor for dancing, music and idling in the sun. I am sullen and angry, mean and moody.

Woe betide those
who cross my path."

"Go away, you prickly hedgehog," said the fish. "Spring is the time for the forest stream to rejoice, for the fish to swim in it and for the crabs to scuttle along its bed and for the frogs on the bank to croak, waiting for the rain. On such a day nobody looks at the sullen and the angry, the mean and the moody."

"I am a prickly hedgehog! I have just woken from a long sleep and I do not care for spring, berries, leaves and climbing, digging gardens and building houses, songs, dancing and idling, nor for the fun in the forest stream. That is why the clouds have brought the rain, the storm and the furious wind, and that is why I can now be sullen and angry, mean and moody to my heart's content.

Nobody will cross me any more!"

Soon the sun began to shine and a colourful rainbow appeared in the sky. A spring flower bloomed in the hedgehog's path. Then a butterfly landed on the flower just as the prickly hedgehog was about to step on it. He hesitated and looked at the flower, the rainbow and the butterfly, taking in all the beauty of the spring. When he finally left, his prickles drooping down, he did not step on the flower or the butterfly, but he smiled joyfully and set off through the field which was full of sweet smells, butterflies and flowers.